For Petra

Published in the United States of America in 2000 by
MONDO Publishing

First published in the United Kingdom
by Julia MacRae Books (The Random House Group UK) 1992

For information contact:
MONDO Publishing
990 Avenue of the Americas
New York, New York 10018

Visit our web site at http://www.mondopub.com

Printed in Hong Kong
First Mondo printing, January 2000
00   01   02   03   04   05   9 8 7 6 5 4 3 2 1
ISBN 1-57255-429-0

Designed by David Neuhaus/NeuStudio, Inc.
Production by The Kids at Our House

Library of Congress Cataloging-in-Publication Data available

Ginger

Ant Parker

MONDO

Ginger likes
to go for a walk...

And to jump on
windowsills...

And to hide
behind bushes...

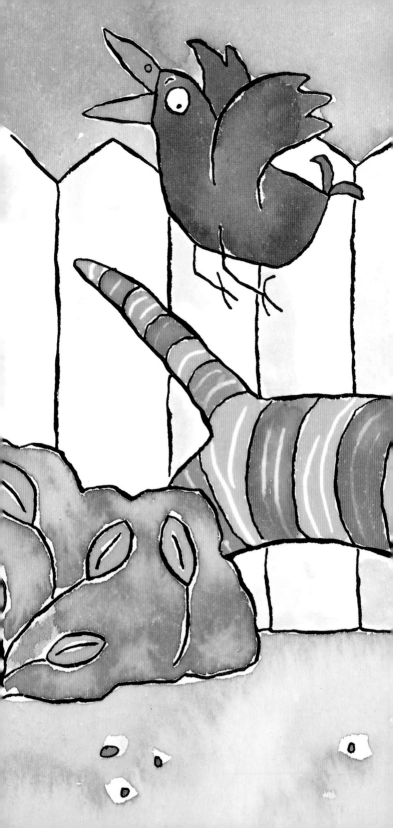

And to play with
the wash...

And to sit by
the pool...

And to meet her friends...

And to tease
the dog...

And to go home!